SEVEN SILLIES

Written by Joyce Dunbar

Illustrated by Chris Downing

AN ARTISTS & WRITERS GUILD BOOK
Golden Books
Western Publishing Company, Inc.
850 Third Avenue, New York, N.Y. 10022

On a bright and shining morning, Pig looked
into the pond.

"There's a pig in the pond," said Pig.
"Such a handsome pig!"
And Pig called over to Sheep.

"What do you see in the pond?" asked Pig.
"I see a pig and a sheep," answered Sheep.
"Such a beautiful sheep!"
And Sheep called over to Goat.

"What do you see in the pond?" asked Sheep.
"I see a pig and a sheep and a goat,"
answered Goat.

"Such a gorgeous goat."
And Goat called over to Rabbit.

"What do you see in the pond?" asked Goat.
"I see a pig and a sheep and a goat and a rabbit,"
answered Rabbit.

"Such a splendid rabbit!"
And Rabbit called over to Hen.

"What do you see in the pond?" asked Rabbit.
"I see a pig and a sheep and a goat and a rabbit
and a hen," said Hen.
"Such a fine, feathered hen."
And Hen called over to Mouse.

"What do you see in the pond?" asked Hen.
"I see a pig and a sheep and a goat and a
rabbit and a hen and a mouse," said Mouse.

"Such a dear, little mouse."
And Mouse called over to Frog.

"What do you see in the pond?" asked Mouse.
"I see seven sillies," answered Frog.
"Seven sillies?" asked the pig and the sheep
and the goat and the rabbit and the hen and
the mouse. "What do you mean?"

"They are all in the pond and they want to get out," said Frog.
"How can we get them out?"
"You will have to jump in and fetch them," answered Frog.

So the pig and the sheep and the goat and the rabbit and the hen and the mouse all jumped into the water with a *splash*!

"There is nothing in the pond, after all!" they said.

"Oh, yes, there is," laughed Frog.
"There is a handsome pig,
a beautiful sheep,
a gorgeous goat,
a splendid rabbit,
a fine, feathered hen,
a dear, little mouse,
and that makes seven sillies."

The animals scrambled out of the pond all
sopping and dripping with water. They
did feel very silly!
Then...
"How many sillies?" asked Pig.

"Seven," said Frog.

Pig began to count. The other animals joined in.

"One, two, three, four, five, six –"

The only one left was Frog.

"Aha!" they laughed. "SEVEN SILLIES!"

"We see a frog that can't count," they said.
"Such a silly frog!"

Library of Congress Cataloging-in-Publication Data

Dunbar, Joyce.
Seven sillies/written by Joyce Dunbar; illustrated by Chris Downing.
p.   cm.
Summary: After Pig, Sheep, Goat, Rabbit, Hen, and Mouse become so enamored of
their reflections in the pond that they jump in, it is Frog who tricked them who ends up
as the silliest of all.
$13.95
[1. Animals—Fiction.   2. Pride and vanity—Fiction.]
I. Downing, Christine, 1931–   ill.   II. Title.   III. Title: 7 sillies.
PZ7.S8944Se   1994

[E]—dc20

93-23083
CIP
AC

First published in Great Britain in 1993 by Andersen Press Ltd.